Enid Blyton's
The Yellow Trumpets

ILLUSTRATED BY K. RAYMOND AND A. GREY

D1211059

A TEMPLAR BOOK

Produced by The Templar Company plc, Pippbrook Mill, London Road, Dorking, Surrey RH4 1JE, Great Britain.

Text copyright © *The Yellow Trumpets* 1926 by Darrell Waters Limited
This edition illustration and design copyright © 1996 by The Templar Company plc
Enid Blyton's signature mark is a registered trademark of Darrell Waters Limited

This edition produced for Parragon Books, Units 13-17, Avonbridge Trading Estate, Atlantic Road, Avonmouth, Bristol BS11 9QD

This book contains material first published as *The Golden Trumpets* in Enid Blyton's Teacher's Treasury 1926.

Printed and bound in Italy

ISBN 0-75251-496-2

•PARRAGON•

Once upon a time there were two little elves who lived in Fairyland and made trumpets. They made all sorts of lovely trumpets – big ones, little ones, long ones, short ones, white ones, red ones and blue ones.

They sold them as fast as they made them, because the baby fairies loved blowing them, and were always coming to buy them.

"One penny, please," said Flip, giving a brownie a red one.

All day long they sold them in their little shop, and when night came they shut the shop and sat down to make more.

Soon every fairy baby, little elf, and tiny pixie had a trumpet, and you should have heard the noise in the streets and houses of Fairyland.

"Tan-tan-tara! Tan-tan-tara!"

It was the baby trumpeters blowing their trumpets.

The older fairies didn't mind at first. They liked the babies to amuse themselves and have fun. They put up with the noise and laughed.

But one day Pinkle discovered a way to make a trumpet which made such a loud noise that any passer-by nearly jumped out of his skin when he heard it!

It was a large, wide, yellow trumpet, beautifully made. Pinkle was very pleased with it.

"Flip!" he called. "Come here, and see my new trumpet!"

Flip hurried to see it. Pinkle showed the trumpet to him, then

hid himself behind the window curtains.

When a gnome came hurrying by the window, carrying his morning's shopping, Pinkle blew his yellow trumpet loudly.

"Tan-tan-tan-TARA!" it went, right in the gnome's ear. He had never in his life heard such a tremendous noise.

He jumped into the air in fright, dropped his basket of shopping, and went scurrying down the street as fast as he could, feeling quite sure that some dreadful animal was roaring at him.

Pinkle and Flip laughed till they cried.

"Let's show the trumpet to the babies!" said Pinkle. "They're sure to want one each, and we will charge them sixpence!"

"Oh yes," said Flip in delight. "Then we will be so rich that we'll

never need to make any more
trumpets, and we'll go
away and have a lazy
time for the rest
of our lives!"

So the two naughty elves
showed the baby fairies their
new trumpet, and told them
what fun they could have
frightening everyone.

The little fairies thought it was a lovely idea, and sounded like great fun, and so did the baby pixies. They asked Pinkle and Flip to make them each one, and agreed that they would pay them sixpence.

So the two elves set to work, and by the next day they had made twelve, and sold them all for sixpence each.

Then what a noise there was in the streets of Fairyland! "Tan-tan-TARA! Tan-tan-TARA!"

The new trumpets nearly deafened everyone, and made people jump in fright.

"This won't do at all," said the King of the fairies. "We must stop this. We don't mind the little trumpets, but these big trumpets are too noisy. Pinkle and Flip must not make any more."

So a message was sent to tell the two elves they must not make any more of the big yellow trumpets.

They were terribly disappointed. What a shame not to make any more, just as they were getting so rich through selling them! Oh dear, oh dear!

Pinkle and Flip talked about the message very crossly, and then Flip suddenly whispered something in Pinkle's big left ear:

"Let's go on making them and selling them anyway. We'll tell the customers to come at night, and no one will know. Shall we, Pinkle?"

Pinkle nodded.

"Yes! We won't take any notice of their silly message. We'll make lots and lots more, and sell them every night when it's dark."

So when their little customers came to the shop, the naughty elves whispered to them to come and buy their yellow trumpets at midnight, if they really badly wanted them.

And night after night naughty little fairies and mischievous little pixies came creeping to Pinkle's back door, paid sixpence, and took away a trumpet.

Pinkle and Flip became
richer and richer, and Fairyland
became noisier and noisier.

At last the older fairies became really angry. They couldn't even sleep at night because of all the noise. But although they watched Pinkle and Flip's shop carefully every single day, they never *once* saw the elves sell one of those big yellow trumpets that made such a dreadful noise. They couldn't understand it. Where *did* the trumpets come from if Pinkle and Flip didn't make them?

"I know what we'll do," said one of the fairies. "We'll go to Flip and Pinkle's shop, and search it from top to bottom. Then we shall know if they have been making the trumpets. If they haven't, we must look somewhere else! We'll go as soon as the shop is open tomorrow!"

Now, that night when a little elf came to buy a trumpet, he told them what he had heard, and the two naughty elves were terribly frightened.

They knew that if they were found out, they might be sent right away from Fairyland, and they didn't want *that* to happen.

"What shall we do, what shall we do?" cried Pinkle. "We've nowhere to hide the trumpets!"

Flip thought for a minute.

"I know," he said, "We'll hide them in the fields. Quick, bring as many as you can!"

The two elves hurried out to the

fields, where a great many yellow flowers were growing.

"If we stick our trumpets into the middle of these yellow flowers, no one will guess where they are!" said Flip. "Come on!"

And quickly he began pushing a big yellow trumpet into each yellow-petalled flower. They matched beautifully!

When all the trumpets were hidden, the two elves went back to

their shop. It was just time to open it, so they unbolted the door.

In came the King of the fairies, and told Pinkle and Flip they were going to search the house from top to bottom.

"Certainly!" said Pinkle politely. "Please do! You won't find a single yellow trumpet here!"

And they didn't! Not one! But just as they were going away again, feeling very puzzled, a pixie came running in.

"Come and see the lovely yellow flowers in the field!" he cried. "They are wonderful! We've never seen anything like them before!"

Off went everyone to see them,

and Pinkle and Flip were taken along too.

But when the fairies looked at them carefully, they saw what made the flowers look strange and beautiful – they each had a yellow trumpet in the midst of their petals!

"So *that's* where you hid them, you rascals!" cried the fairies, and caught hold of Pinkle and Flip angrily. "Out of Fairyland you shall go!"

"No, no!" wept Pinkle and Flip

miserably. "Please let us stay. We'll never, *never*, NEVER make big yellow trumpets again!"

Suddenly a fairy had a great idea.

"I know!" he cried. "Let's allow Pinkle and Flip to go on making their trumpets for these flowers! See how much more beautiful they are with the long trumpets in the middle!"

"Yes, yes!" cried all the fairies and pixies.

So it was settled. And from that day to this, Pinkle and Flip had to work hard to make the big yellow trumpets for the loveliest yellow flowers of the spring.

You have seen them often, for
daffodils grow in everybody's
garden – and if you look carefully
at them next springtime, you will
see how beautifully Pinkle and Flip
have made their yellow trumpets.